D0938170

IRON HANS

BY THE BROTHERS GRIMM

ILLUSTRATED BY

Marilee Heyer

VIKING

Also by Marilee Heyer

The Weaving of a Dream
The Forbidden Door

The artwork was done in colored pencil
on 100% rag illustration board.

VIKING
Published by the Penguin Group
Penguin Books USA Inc., 375 Hudson Street, New York, New York 10014, U.S.A.
Penguin Books Ltd, 27 Wrights Lane, London W8 5TZ, England
Penguin Books Australia Ltd, Ringwood, Victoria, Australia
Penguin Books Canada Ltd, 10 Alcorn Avenue, Toronto, Ontario, Canada M4V 3B2
Penguin Books (N.Z.) Ltd, 182–190 Wairau Road, Auckland 10, New Zealand

Penguin Books Ltd, Registered Offices: Harmondsworth, Middlesex, England

First published in 1993 by Viking, a division of Penguin Books USA Inc.

1 3 5 7 9 10 8 6 4 2

Library of Congress Cataloging-in-Publication Data
Eisenhans. English. Iron Hans / the Brothers Grimm ;
illustrated by Marilee Heyer. p. cm.
Summary: With the help of Iron Hans, the wild man
of the forest, a young prince makes his own way
in the world and wins the hand of a princess.
ISBN 0-670-81741-4
[1. Fairy tales. 2. Folklore — Germany.]
I. Grimm, Jacob, 1785–1863. II. Grimm, Wilhelm, 1786–1859.
III. Heyer, Marilee, ill. IV. Title.
PZ8.E37Ir 1993 398.21 — dc20 [E] 93-14662 CIP AC

Printed in Singapore Set in 14 point Cochin

With my love and gratitude to
RON BOUDREAU,
whose dear childhood portraits, and my memories of him,
were the inspiration for the young prince

And to
ROB CORDER,
for designing the cover type for my last two books
and for patiently helping me through the creative process

And to their wives,
LINDA BOUDREAU and LONNA CORDER,
for recognizing the gold in their hair
and for being pretty golden themselves.

—M. H.

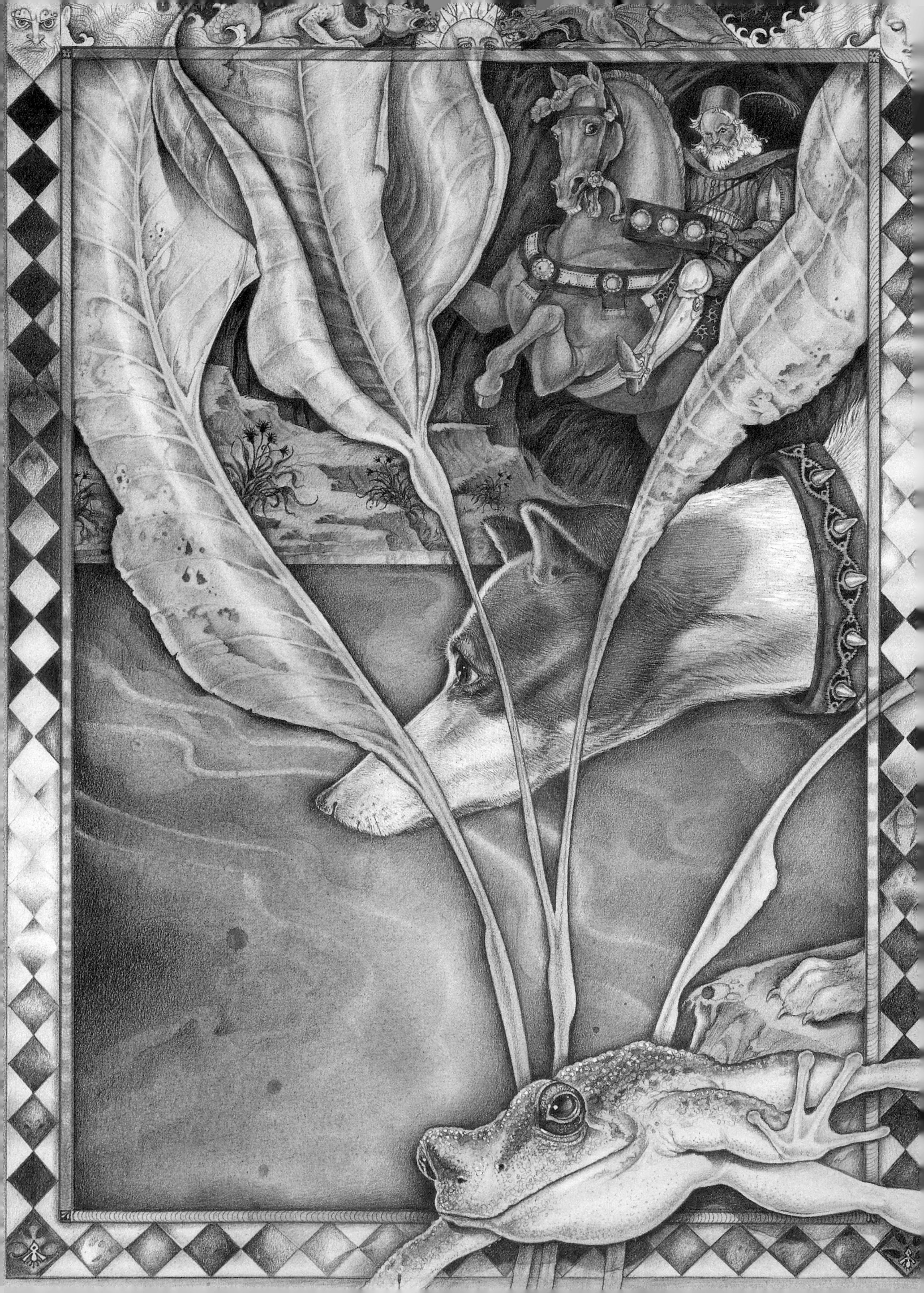

Once upon a time there was a king who owned a great wood which lay behind his castle and was filled with wild game; the king loved to hunt there. One day, one of his huntsmen who had gone into this wood in the morning did not return.

The next morning, the king sent two other huntsmen to find him and they, too, did not return. Finally the king ordered all his huntsmen to search the entire forest to find their missing companions. But none of them ever returned, not even a single dog out of the whole pack that accompanied them.

The king issued a law forbidding anyone to enter the forest. And from that day onward, a deep silence and stillness fell over the whole forest, broken only by the occasional call of an owl or the glimpse of an eagle flying above it.

This went on for a long time, until one day a strange huntsman came before the king, asking for an audience. He told the king that he was ready to go into the dangerous forest. The king would not at first give his consent, saying, "I am afraid you will fare no better than the others, and that you will never return."

"I will dare the danger," the huntsman replied, "for I know nothing of fear."

So it was that the huntsman entered the forest with his dog. In a few minutes the hound saw a wild animal and began to pursue it. But it had scarcely gone a few yards before it came to the edge of a deep pool, from which a naked arm stretched itself and, catching the dog, drew it down under the water.

The huntsman, seeing this, quickly went back to the castle and brought back with him three men with pails to bail out the water. When they came to the bottom they found a wild man whose body was brown like rusty iron, with hair hanging over his face down to his knees. The men bound him with cords and led him away to the king, who ordered an immense iron cage to be built in the courtyard and the wild man placed inside. The queen was given responsibility for the key, and the king further ordered that anyone opening the cage would be punished by death. Now people were free to go into the forest again.

One day, the king's son, who was eight years old, was playing in the courtyard. Suddenly his golden ball accidentally rolled into the iron cage. He ran up to the bars of the cage and demanded that the wild man return his ball.

"Not till you open my door," answered the wild man.

"No, I cannot," said the boy, "for my father the king has forbidden it."

And then he ran back inside the castle.

But the next morning the boy came again and demanded his golden ball.

"Open my door," said the wild man, but the boy refused.

The third morning the king went out hunting in the forest, and soon the boy came again to the cage and said, "Even if I wanted to open the door, I haven't got the key to do it."

"It is under your mother's pillow," said the wild man, "and you can get it if you like."

So the boy, thinking only of his wish to have his ball, ran and fetched the key. The door swung heavily, and the boy pinched his finger, but soon it opened and the wild man, giving him the golden ball, stepped out and hurried off.

At this the boy became alarmed and burst into tears, calling, "Wild man, do not go away or I shall be beaten!"

The wild man turned back and, raising the boy up, set him upon his shoulders and walked swiftly into the forest.

Soon afterward, the king returned to his castle, where he saw the empty cage in the courtyard and asked the queen what had happened. She called for her son, but there was no reply. The king sent people out over the fields to search for him, but they returned empty-handed. Then the king knew for certain what had really happened, and the entire court was stricken with grief.

Meanwhile, as soon as the wild man had reached the forest again, he took the boy down off his shoulders, set him on his feet, and said to him, "You will never see your father and mother again. But I will keep you with me, for you freed me and I have compassion for you. If you do all that I tell you, you will be well treated, for I have enough treasure and gold — in fact, more than anyone else in the world."

That night Iron Hans made a bed of moss for the boy to sleep on, and the next morning he took him to a pool. "This golden water is as bright and clear as crystal," he said. "Here you must sit, and make sure that nothing falls into it, or it will be polluted. I will come each evening to make sure that you have obeyed my commands."

So the boy sat down on the bank of the pool. At times he glimpsed a golden fish or a gold snake within its depths. As he had been instructed, he took care that nothing fell in. But his finger still hurt so badly from opening the cage that before he realized it, he had dipped it into the water to cool it. He quickly drew his finger out again, but too late, for he saw that his finger had turned to gold! No matter how hard he tried, he couldn't rub it off.

In the evening Iron Hans returned, and after looking at the boy, he asked, "What has happened to my pool?"

"Nothing, nothing!" the boy replied, hiding his finger behind him.

But Iron Hans said, "You have dipped your finger into the water. This once, however, I will overlook it. Take care that it does not happen again."

The next day the boy took up his post at the pond. Soon his finger ached again, and this time he put it to his head and happened to pull off a hair which fell into the water. He took it out again very quickly, but it had changed into gold.

When Iron Hans came again he said, "You have let a hair fall into the pool, and once more I will overlook your fault. But if it happens again the pool will be polluted, and you can remain with me no longer."

On the third morning the boy sat by the pond, taking care not to move his finger despite the pain. The time passed so slowly that he began to look at his face reflected in the mirror of the waters, and the desire came to him to look straight into his own eyes. Closer and closer to the water he leaned, and suddenly his long hair fell down from his shoulders into the pool. Swiftly he straightened, but all of the hair on his head had turned to gold and shone like the sun itself.

Terrified, the boy quickly took out his handkerchief and wrapped his head, so that his hair would be concealed from the wild man. But as soon as Iron Hans returned he knew everything and said, "Untie your handkerchief!"

Then the boy's golden hair fell free upon his shoulders and all his excuses were in vain. "You have not stood the test," said Iron Hans, "and so cannot remain here any longer. Go forth into the world, and there you will see how it is to be poor. But there's no wickedness in your heart, and I mean well toward you, so I will grant you this one favor: when you are in trouble, come to this forest and call, 'Iron Hans.' I will come out and help you. My power is great, greater than you know, and I have gold and silver in abundance."

So the king's son had to leave the forest, and he walked along beaten and unbeaten paths, ever onward, until he came at length to a large town. There he sought work, but without success, for in his early years he had learned nothing which was of use. At last he went to the palace there and asked if they could take him in. The court servants knew of no vacancies he could fill, but because he seemed a likely lad they allowed him to remain. Before too long the cook took him into his service and told him he might fetch wood and water for the fire and sweep up the ashes.

One day, when no one else was at hand, the prince had to carry in a dish for the royal table. But because he would not allow his golden hair to be seen, he entered the room with his cap on his head.

When the king saw him he exclaimed, "If you come to the royal table, you must pull off your cap!"

"Ah, Your Majesty, I do not dare," the prince replied. "I have a bad disease on my head."

The king then ordered the cook to come before him and scolded him because he had taken such a youth into his service, and finally commanded that the cook fire him.

But the cook pitied the poor lad and made him change places with the gardener's boy.

Now the prince had to plant and sow, to dig and chop, in wind and rain and every sort of weather. One day, when it was summer, as he was working alone in the garden, he took off his cap to cool his head in the breeze; the sun shone so brightly upon his hair that the golden locks glittered and flashed, and their brilliant rays shone into the chamber of the king's daughter.

Up she jumped to see what it was, and, seeing the gardener's boy, called to him to bring her a nosegay of flowers.

Quickly he put on his cap and gathered some wildflowers, taking the time to arrange them. But as he was going up the steps to take them to the princess, the gardener met him and said, "How can you give the princess such an ordinary bouquet? Go back and fetch the rarest and the most beautiful blossoms."

"Oh, no," said the boy. "The wildflowers bloom the longest and will please the best."

So he went up to the princess's chamber, and she said to him, "Take off your cap. It isn't proper for you to wear it here!"

The boy, however, replied that he dared not remove it, because his head was too ugly to look at. But the princess seized his cap and pulled it off, and his golden hair fell down over his shoulders, a beautiful sight. The boy would have run away, but the princess detained him and gave him a handful of gold coins. Then he left and took her money to the gardener, telling him to give it to his children to play with, for he despised money.

The following day the princess called to him again, asking for a bouquet of wildflowers, and when he entered her chamber with them she reached again to take his cap. But this time he held it fast with both hands and would not let it go.

"Here," the princess said, and gave him still another handful of gold coins. But the boy would not keep them, and gave them to the gardener's children for playthings.

The third day it was just the same. The princess could not get his cap and he would not keep her coins.

A short while later, the country was drawn into a war. The king collected all his men, not knowing if he would be able to make a stand against the enemy, which was very powerful and led an immense army.

The gardener's boy asked for a horse, saying that he was grown up and ready to take his part in the fight. People laughed. "When we are gone we will leave a horse for you," someone told him.

So as soon as the rest had set out, the young prince went into the stable and found the horse there. It was lame, and its feet clicked together as it went. Nevertheless, he mounted it and rode away to the gloomy forest.

As soon as he arrived, he called out loudly, "Iron Hans! Iron Hans!"

Soon the wild man appeared and asked, "What is it that you desire?"

"I desire a strong horse, for I am going to battle," said the youth.

"That you shall have, and more than you desire," said Iron Hans, and disappeared back into the forest.

From among the trees a page came forward, holding a horse so fiery that he was scarcely to be touched. Behind the steed followed a great troop of warriors, all clad in iron, with swords that glittered in the sun.

The youth then mounted the fiery horse and rode off at the head of his army. Just as he reached the field of battle, he found the greater part of the king's army already slain and the rest on the point of yielding. The youth charged at once with his iron army, like a storm of hail, and they cut down all who opposed them. The enemy turned and fled, but the young prince pursued and killed all the fugitives, so that not one man was left. Then, instead of leading his troop before the king, he rode back with them to the forest and summoned Iron Hans, who asked, "What do you desire now?"

"Take back all these soldiers and your steed," said the youth. "And give back to me my lame horse." All this was done as he desired, and he rode home on his limping animal.

When the king returned to his castle, his daughter greeted him and congratulated him on his victory.

"I do not deserve it," the king said. "We owe our victory to a strange knight who came to our aid with his soldiers." His daughter inquired who he was, but the king told her he did not know. Then the princess asked the gardener about his boy. He told her that the lad had just returned home on his lame steed. The others had laughed at him, saying, "Here comes Hop-a-da-hop! What hedge did *you* hide behind?" Replied the boy, "I have done the best I could, and without me you would have fared badly." At this speech they all mocked him even more.

Some time after this the king said to his daughter, "I'm ordering that a great festival be held, which shall last three days. You shall throw a golden apple, for which, perhaps, the unknown knight will contend."

As soon as the proclamation was made, the young prince went to the forest and called for Iron Hans, who asked, "What do you desire?"

"That I may catch the golden apple."

"It is all the same as if you had it now," said Iron Hans. "But you shall have a red suit of armor, and shall ride there upon a chestnut horse."

When the appointed day came, the young man took his place among the other knights and was not recognized by anyone. The princess stepped forward and tossed up the golden apple, which no man was able to catch but the red knight, who rode away as soon as he obtained it.

The second day Iron Hans gave him a suit of white armor and a gray horse, and again he alone caught the apple.

The king was angry when the knight rode away with the prize, and said, "That is not right. He must appear before me and declare his name." Then he ordered that if the knight who caught the apple the next day failed to give his name, someone should pursue him and, if he would not return willingly, cut him down or stab him.

On the third day Iron Hans gave the prince a black suit of armor and a black steed, and again the prince caught the apple when it was thrown. When he rode away, the king's men pursued him, and one came close enough to wound him in the leg with the point of his weapon. Still he escaped them; but his horse jumped so violently that his helmet fell from his head and his golden hair was seen by all. The king's men rode back and told the king all that had occurred.

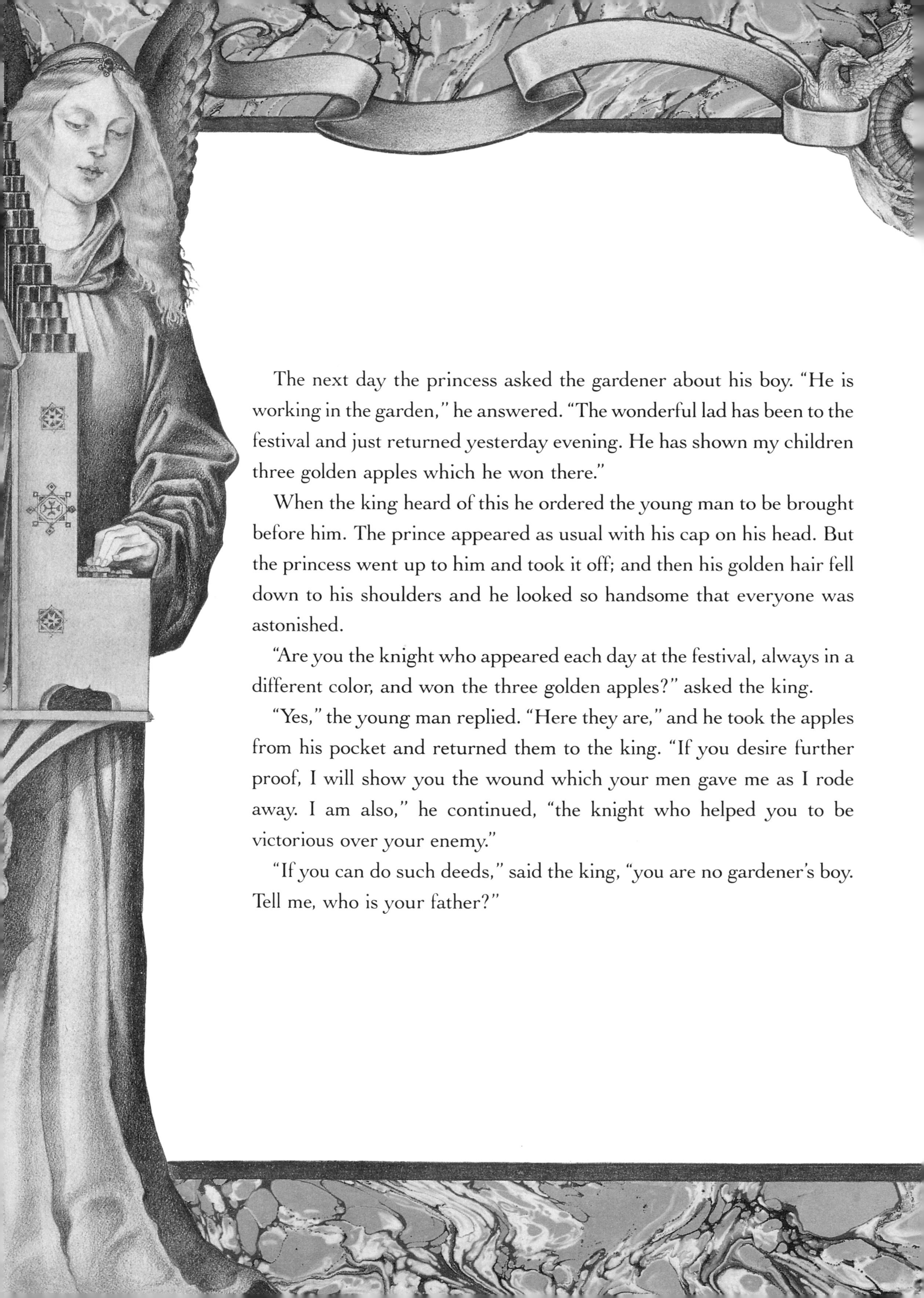

The next day the princess asked the gardener about his boy. "He is working in the garden," he answered. "The wonderful lad has been to the festival and just returned yesterday evening. He has shown my children three golden apples which he won there."

When the king heard of this he ordered the young man to be brought before him. The prince appeared as usual with his cap on his head. But the princess went up to him and took it off; and then his golden hair fell down to his shoulders and he looked so handsome that everyone was astonished.

"Are you the knight who appeared each day at the festival, always in a different color, and won the three golden apples?" asked the king.

"Yes," the young man replied. "Here they are," and he took the apples from his pocket and returned them to the king. "If you desire further proof, I will show you the wound which your men gave me as I rode away. I am also," he continued, "the knight who helped you to be victorious over your enemy."

"If you can do such deeds," said the king, "you are no gardener's boy. Tell me, who is your father?"

"My father is a mighty king. I have all the gold I desire, and more than can even be imagined."

"Truly," the king said, "I am indebted to you. Can I do anything to show it?"

"Yes, you can give me your daughter to wife," answered the young man.

The princess laughed, and said, "He doesn't make a short story long. But I saw long ago that he was no gardener's boy from his golden hair." So saying, she went and kissed him.

By and by the wedding was celebrated, and to it came the prince's father and mother, who had long ago given up their son for dead and had lost all hope of seeing him again.

While they all sat at the bridal feast, suddenly music was heard, and the doors opened to reveal a proud king entering, attended by a great retinue. He went up to the young prince and embraced him. "I am Iron Hans," he said. "An enchantment made me a wild man, but you have set me free. All the treasures which belong to me are now yours!"